STERLING CHILDREN'S BOOKS
New York

An Imprint of Sterling Publishing Co., Inc.
1166 Avenue of the Americas
New York, NY 10036

ISBN 978-1-4549-3568-1

Distributed in Canada by Sterling Publishing Co., Inc.
c/o Canadian Manda Group, 664 Annette Street
Toronto, Ontario M6S 2C8, Canada

For information about custom editions, special sales, and premium
and corporate purchases, please contact Sterling Special Sales at 800-805-5489 or
specialsales@sterlingpublishing.com.

Manufactured in China

Lot #:
2 4 6 8 10 9 7 5 3 1
06/19

sterlingpublishing.com

Cover and interior design by Irene Vandervoort
Illustrations by Joseph Ewers

People in Your Neighborhood

STERLING CHILDREN'S BOOKS
New York

Oh, who are the people
in your neighborhood,

In your neighborhood,
In your neighborhood?

Say, who are the people in your neighborhood,
The people that you meet each day?

Oh, hi there, little fella.

Hey, listen,
you know who you could be
if I gave you this little hat
and a bag to carry
over your shoulder?

Hello.

Then I could be a
laundryman.

No, not a laundryman.

How about
Santa Claus?

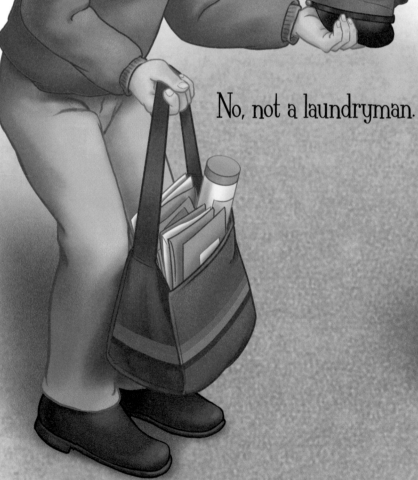

Oh, the postman always brings the mail,

Through rain or snow or sleet or hail.

I'll work and work the whole day through
To get your letters safe to you.

'Cause a postman is a person in your neighborhood,
In your neighborhood,
He's in your neighborhood.

A postman is a person in your neighborhood,
A person that you meet each day.

No, not Santa Claus.

No? Little Red Riding Hood?

No, no, no,
not Red Riding Hood.
You could be a fireman!

A fireman? Holy smoke!

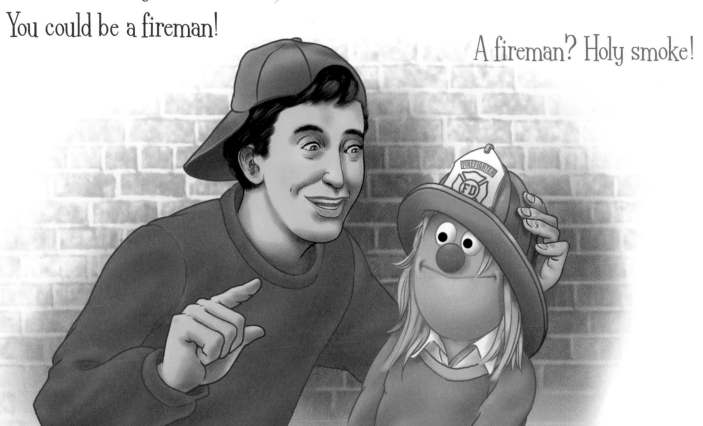

Oh, a fireman is brave, it's said.
His engine is a shiny red.

If there's a fire anywhere about,
Well, I'll be sure to put it out.

'Cause a fireman is a person in your neighborhood,
In your neighborhood,
He's in your neighborhood.

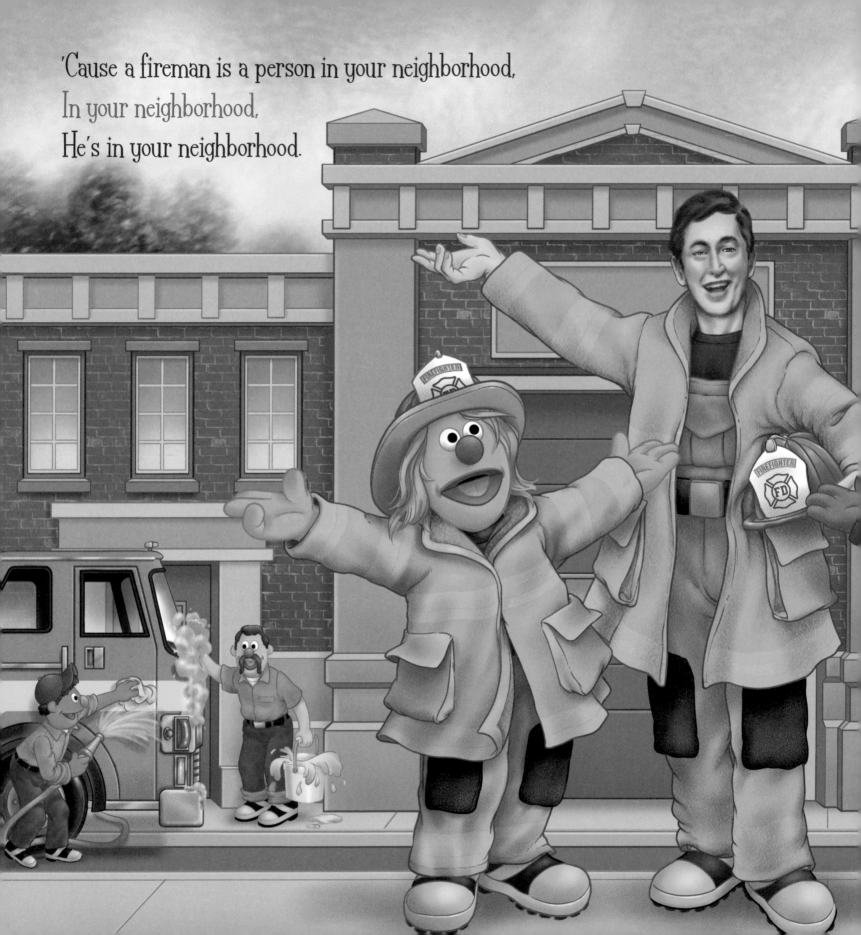

And a postman is a person in your neighborhood.
Well, they're the people that you meet
when you're walking down the street,
they're the people that you meet each day.

Who are some of the other people
in your neighborhood?

Baker
A baker is someone who bakes
things in an oven, usually all
kinds of breads and cookies.

Dentist
A dentist is someone who helps
you take care of your teeth.

Veterinarian
A veterinarian is someone who takes care of animals when they get sick.

Librarian
A librarian is someone who works at the library and can help you find books.